Sid Fleischman

McBROOM
Tells a Lie

Illustrated by Walter Lorraine

MCBROOM TELLS A LIE
0-590-98289-3

(For I.D. purposes only)

ISBN 0-590-98289-3

Text copyright © 1976 by Albert S. Fleischman.
Illustrations copyright © 1976 by Walter H. Lorraine.
All rights reserved. Published by Scholastic Inc., 555 Broadway, New York, NY 10012, by arrangement with Little, Brown and Company (Inc.).

12 11 10 9 8 7 6 5 4 3 2 1   8 9/9 0 1 2 3/0

Printed in the U.S.A.

For
Andy Carpenter

It's true — I did tell a lie once.

I don't mean the summer nights we hung caged chickens in the farmhouse for lanterns. Those hens had eaten so many lightning bugs they glowed brighter'n kerosene lamps.

And I don't mean the cold snap that came along so sudden that blazing sunshine froze to the ground. We pickaxed chunks of it for the stove to cook on.

That's the genuine truth, sure and certain as my name's Josh McBroom.

The time I told a lie — well, I'd best start with the spring day the young'uns came home from school. They were lugging an old black stovepipe, which they put in the barn.

The next day they dragged home a broken buggy wheel. They put that in the barn, too.

Gracious! It wasn't long before that barn was filling up with empty coffee cans, scrap pieces of lumber, tin funnels, busted chairs, a rusted bicycle and all manner of throwaway stuff.

Then they began a-sawing and a-hammering and hardly came out of the barn to eat. They were building a hoopdedoodle of some sort. The scamps kept it covered with a sheet. I reckoned they'd tell us when they were ready.

"Will*jill*hester*chester*peter*polly*tim*tom-*

mary*larry*andlittle*clarinda!*" my dear wife Melissa called out every evening. "Supper!"

We had hardly sat down to eat one night when Jill asked, "Pa, would Mexican jumping beans grow on our farm?"

I hadn't seen anything yet that wouldn't grow on our wonderful one-acre farm. That trifling patch of earth was so amazing rich we could plant and harvest two-three crops a day — with time left over for a game of horseshoes. Why, just last month Little Clarinda dropped her silver baby fork and by time we found it the thing had grown into a silver pitchfork.

"Mexican jumping beans?" I answered. "I don't think they make good eating."

"We don't want them to eat," Will said.

"Will you let us grow a crop?" Polly asked. "We need bushels and bushels."

"For our invention," Tom put in.

"In that case," I said, "jump to it, my lambs."

They traded with a boy at school who owned a jar of the hopping beans. First thing Saturday morning they lit out the back door to plant their crop.

And along came our foxy-eyed neighbor, Heck Jones. You never saw such a spare-ribbed and rattleboned man. Why, he was so skinny he could slip through a knothole without tipping his hat. He wore a diamond stickpin in his tie and was swinging a bamboo cane. Our dog, Zip, stood barking at him.

"Josh McBroom," he said. "I'm here to do some trading."

"Trade what?"

"My big farm for yours — even. You can keep the dog."

"No sir and nohow," I said. His farm was

9

so worn out he had to plant his own weeds.

He leaned both hands heavily on his bamboo cane. *"Hee-haw!"* he snickered. "Reckon I'll get your land, neighbor — one way or t'other."

And off he ambled up the road, *hee-haw-ing* through his nose. He'd been visiting almighty often lately. I stomped over the hole his cane had left in the ground. I had to be careful not to let holes get a good start in our rich topsoil — the blamed things grow.

Meanwhile the young'uns had laid out the rows and began sowing the beans.

Well, that was a mistake. I should have known that our soil was too powerful strong for jumping beans. The seeds sprouted faster'n the twitch of a sheep's tail and those Mexican bushes shot up lickety-bang. As they quick-dried in the prairie sun the pods began to shake and rattle and Chester shouted: "Pa, look!"

Merciful powers! Those buzzing, jumping, wiggle-waggling pods jerked the roots clear out of the ground. And off those bushes went, leaping and hopping every which way.

"Willjillhesterchesterpeterpollytimtom-

marylarryandlittleclarinda!" I called out. "After them, my lambs!"

Didn't those plants lead us on a merry chase! A good many got clean away, hopping and bucking and rattling across the countryside. But we did manage to capture enough for the young'uns' invention.

They were shelling the beans when the

dog reared up barking. Heck Jones was back with four scrawny hens and a bob-tailed rooster out for a walk.

"Howdy, neighbor," he said. "I'm here to do some trading. My farm for yours and I'll throw in this flock of fat hens. My prize rooster, too. You can keep the dog."

I looked at those sorry fowl, scratching and pecking away in the dirt. "No sir and nohow," I said. "Our farm's not for trade, Heck Jones."

"*Hee-haw*, I'll get it one way or t'other," he said, tipping his hat toward the end of his nose. "Good day, neighbor."

It was the next morning, before breakfast, when the young'uns finished tinkering with their invention. They called my dear wife Melissa and me out to the barn and whipped off the sheet.

Glory be! There stood an odds and ends

contraption on four wheels. A rain barrel was mounted in front with three tin funnels sticking out of the top. The scamps had fixed up their collection of broken chairs to seat all eleven of them.

"We're going to call it a Jumping Beanmobile," Jill said.

"If it runs we won't have to walk all that five miles to school and back," said Peter.

"My stars," Mama declared.

"Pile in, everybody," Will said, "and let's start 'er up."

The young'uns flocked to their seats. Will, Jill and Hester began pouring beans into the funnels.

Mercy! You never heard such a racket inside that rain barrel. The beans began to hop, jump and leap something fearful, bouncing against tin cans from the sound of things. I found out later the cans were fitted into stovepipe — looked something like the cylinders on my broken-down Franklin automobile. They had the things

hooked up to the front wheels with bicycle
chains.

"More fuel!" Will called out, and more

jumping beans poured down the funnels.

I declare. The next moment the Jumping Beanmobile clanked forward — a full inch.

"More beans!" Polly shouted happily.

But tarnation! The barrel was already so hopping full that beans were leaping like fleas out of the tops of the funnels.

The young'uns sat there with the smiles dropping from their faces, one by one.

"A splendid invention, my lambs," I said. "Why, all you need is a stronger fuel."

"Hee-haw." Heck Jones had come up behind us and was helping himself to the water dipper. "That infernal machine'll never run, neighbors. Make good firewood, though."

The young'uns rolled their Jumping Beanmobile back into the barn. I was feeling mighty low for them, the way Heck

Jones made fun of them. He was cackling so that he spilled most of the dipper of water on his shoes.

"McBroom, you drive a hard bargain. I'll

trade you my farm, a flock of fat hens, my prize rooster and two plump hogs. You can keep your farm dog."

Plump? Those hogs of his were so puny they could hide behind a broomstick.

"No sir and nohow," I said.

"I'll get what I'm after one way or t'other," he *hee-hawed*, and ambled out of sight around the barn.

When the young'uns came in to breakfast they said they'd seen him scraping the mud off his shoes into an old flour sack.

"By thunder!" I exclaimed. "That's why the confounded rascal's been paying us so many visits."

The older young'uns were standing at the stove breaking fresh eggs into skillets. "Pa — there's something wrong with these breakfast eggs," said Will.

But I was hardly listening. "Why, Heck

20

Jones doesn't intend to trade for our farm," I declared.

"Pa, come look," said Jill from the stove.

"Valuable as gold dust, our topsoil. And he's been stealing it! Yup, out of that hollow bamboo cane he pokes in the earth. And off his wet shoes. And out of the craws of the chickens he brings along to peck dirt!"

"Pa — come quick, but stand back!" my dear wife Melissa exclaimed.

I hopped to the stove as she broke another fresh egg into a skillet. Why, soon as it was fried on one side that egg jumped up in the air. It flipped over and landed on the other side to fry.

"Well, don't that beat all," I said. "The hens must have been eating your Mexican jumping beans. Yup, and they're laying eggs that *flip* themselves. An amazing invention, my lambs!"

But they wouldn't be cheered up by the flip-flopping eggs. A gloom was on them because they wouldn't be riding to school in their Beanmobile.

I scratched my head most of the day. It wouldn't do any good to fence the farm to keep Heck Jones off. You might as well put up a windbreak out of chicken wire.

The young'uns were still feeling almighty low and downsome at supper when my dear wife Melissa tried to jolly everybody up. "Let's pop some corn."

Well, a strange look came over all those sad faces. "Popcorn," Jill whispered.

"Popcorn!" said Hester, beginning to smile.

"POPCORN!" Will laughed. "Bet that'll run our machine!"

Didn't those kids light out for the barn

in a hurry! In no time at all they were clanking and hammering to do over the Beanmobile into a Popcornmobile.

They were still at it the next day, after school, when Heck Jones came running with his shoes off. I reckoned he planned to steal pinches of our farm between his toes.

"I'll have the law on you, McBroom!"

Egg was dripping off his nose and chin. "Do tell," I said coldly.

"You grew them jumping beans, didn't you?"

"Best ever. Looks like your hens pecked 'em down and you didn't step back from the egg skillet fast enough."

"Hang them blasted eggs. Look there at my blue ribbon cow, Princess Prunella!"

My eyes near shot out of my head. There on the horizon that stupid, worthless cow

of his was leaping and high-jumping and bucking.

"Kicked holes right through the barn roof!" Heck Jones snorted. "You allowed them dangerous bushes of yours to get loose and now Princess Prunella's stomachs are full of jumping beans — all four of em!"

"Didn't know she was royalty," I said. "Got her name changed kind of sudden."

"That cow's ruined. It would take ten men on ladders to try and milk her. Worth a fortune, Princess Prunella was, with all her blue ribbons."

I knew for a fact that dumb cow hadn't won a ribbon in her life — but she did eat several once at the county fair.

"Reckon I'll have to shoot her before she does any more damage," he said, beginning to dab at his eyes. "Poor creature."

Well, all that dabbing didn't fool me.

Heck Jones could peel an acre of onions without dropping a tear. But I reckoned I was responsible for all the mischief, letting those bushes get away from us.

"Sir," I said. "If you'll guarantee not to set foot on this farm I'll pay for a barn roof. And I'll buy that ignorant cow from you. I reckon when she settles down she'll give churned butter for a month. Mighty valuable now, Prunella is."

"She ain't for sale!" Heck Jones snapped. "Don't think you're going to slip out so light and easy. I intend to see you in jail, McBroom! Farming with intent to poison up my livestock with crazy-beans. Unless . . ."

"I'm listening, sir."

He cleared his throat. "Neighbor, I'm a kindly man. If you want to trade farms we'll call it fair and square."

"Well, no sir and nohow," I said. "And if I weren't a kindly man I'd have the sheriff after you for trying to steal our topsoil, trifle by trifle."

He caught his hat as a wind sprang up and flapped his coattails. "Slander, sir! I'll have the law on you double. Anyway, you can't prove it!"

"Why, the proof is right between your toes."

He looked down at his feet. "Dear, dear me," he grinned. "I declare if I wasn't in such a rush I forgot my shoes."

"And your hollow bamboo cane."

"Well now, neighbor, we ought to be able to settle things between ourselves." He lifted his thin nose into the wind — that man could sniff things miles off. "Why, you just grow me a crop of tomatoes to make up for my barn roof and we'll forget the rest."

"I'll deliver 'em before supper."

"No, neighbor. Can't use 'em yet. Gotta find a buyer at a good price." He whipped out a pencil and piece of paper. "I'll just write out the agreement. Best to do things honest and legal. You deliver the tomatoes when I say so — fresh off the vine, mind you — and I'll guarantee not to set foot on your farm again."

Glory be! We'd be rid of that petty scoundrel at last.

"But fair's fair, McBroom. I'm entitled to a guarantee too. I'll just put down that if you don't live up to the bargain — why, this useless, worn-out one-acre farm is mine. Sign here."

Useless? Worn-out? My pride rose up and arched like a cat's back. I could raise a crop of tomatoes in an hour. The *hee-haw* would be on him. I signed.

"And no more skulking around, sir," I said.

"A bargain's a bargain," he nodded solemnly. But as he ambled off I thought I heard him snicker through his nose.

It was about sunset when the young'uns rolled their Popcornmobile out of the barn. "It's finished, Pa," Will said.

They had attached black tin stovepipe

underneath the floorboards with bailing wire. It made a mighty stout-looking exhaust pipe.

"And look, Pa," Larry said. "We got headlights, just like your broken-down Franklin."

Indeed they did! Two quart canning jars were fixed to the front. And the scamps had filled the jars with lightning bugs!

"Pa," Mary said. "Can we have a chunk of frozen sunlight out of the icehouse?"

"Not much left," I replied. "But help yourself."

By early candlelight they had dropped a clod of sunlight in the barrel together with a dozen ears of corn. They piled into the seats and waited for the sunshine to thaw and pop the corn and start the machinery clanking.

My dear wife Melissa hurried out to take the sheets off the line — the prairie wind was turning a mite gritty — and there stood Heck Jones.

"Evenin', neighbors," he said. There was a tricksy look in his eye and a piece of paper in his hand. "McBroom, you guaranteed a crop of tomatoes on demand. Well, I'm demanding 'em *now*."

My eyebrows jumped. "Drat it, you can see the sun's down!" I declared.

"There's nothing about the sun in the contract. You read it."

"And it's going to kick up a dust storm before long."

"Nothing in the contract about a dust storm. You signed it."

"Sir, you expect me to grow you a crop of tomatoes *at night in a dust storm?*"

"*Hee-haw,* neighbor. If you don't, this farm's mine. I'll give you till sunup. Not a moment later, McBroom!"

And off he went, chuckling and snickering and *hee-hawing* through his nose.

"Oh, Pa," my dear wife Melissa cried. Even the young'uns were getting a mite onion-eyed.

My heart had sunk somewhere down around my socks, only lower. "Tarnation!" I said. "That rascal's slippery as an eel dipped in lard."

Just then corn began popping like firecrackers inside the young'uns' rain barrel.

"Pa, we're moving!" Jill exclaimed.

Sure enough, the chunk of frozen sunlight had thawed out and the corn was exploding from the stored-up heat.

I tried to raise a smile. Will grabbed the steering wheel tight and began driving the young'uns around the barn. Popcorn shot out of the exhaust pipe, white as snow.

We didn't have enough of that frozen sunshine left to grow a crop, worst luck! But when I saw those two headlights coming around the barn my heart leaped back in place. The jars full of fireflies lit up the way like it was high noon!

"Willjillhesterchesterpeterpollytimtom-marylarryandlittleclarinda!" I shouted. "Fetch canning jars. Fill 'em up with lightning bugs. Quick, my lambs. Not a moment to waste."

The Popcornmobile sputtered to a stop, spitting out the last corncobs from the tailpipe.

Chester said, "The critters have got kind of scarce around here, Pa."

"The thickest place is way the other side of Heck Jones's place," Mary said.

"At Seven-Mile Meadow," Polly nodded.

"A powerful long walk," said Larry.

"Who said anything about walking?" I laughed. "You've got your Popcornmobile, haven't you?"

Didn't we get busy! The young'uns fetched all the canning jars in the cellar and bushels of corn for fuel. With a fresh chunk of frozen sunshine in the barrel off they took — spraying popcorn behind them.

I set to work planting tomato seeds. It was full dark, but I could see fine. My dear wife Melissa held up a chicken by the feet — one of those lantern-glowing hens I was telling you about.

Then I began pounding stakes in the ground for the tomatoes to climb up. It was slow work with the wind blowing grit in my eyes.

"I do hope the young'uns don't get lost,"

my dear wife Melissa said. "It's going to blow a real dust storm by morning."

"Heck Jones had sniffed it coming," I declared. "But lost? Not our scamps. I can hear 'em now. And see 'em too — look!"

They were still a long way off but those headlights glowed bright as sunrise. And that Popcornmobile sounded like the Fourth of July, loud enough to wake snakes.

Jill had taken a turn at the wheel and steered toward the barn. All the kids were waving and laughing. I reckoned that was the best ride they'd ever had.

"That's a jim-dandy machine you built," I smiled. "And I see you found a lightning bug or two."

"Thicker'n mosquitoes, over at Seven-Mile Meadow," Polly said.

Well, it didn't take long to hang those jars of fireflies on the tomato stakes. And glory be! They lit up the farm bright as day.

It wasn't a moment before the tomato sprouts came busting up through the earth.

They broke into leaf and the vines started toward those canning jars. I do believe they preferred that homemade sunshine!

In fact, before we could harvest the crop, pull the stakes and plug the holes, a good many of those tomatoes got sunscald!

We loaded up the Popcornmobile with bushel baskets of tomatoes and I fetched one of the last chunks of frozen sunshine from the icehouse. Will threw a dozen ears of corn into the engine and I went along for the ride.

We made so many trips to Heck Jones's place the popcorn piled up along the road like a snowbank. Finally, minutes before dawn, I hammered at his door.

"Wake up, Heck Jones!" I called.

"Hee-haw!" He began to laugh so hard you'd think he'd swallowed a feather duster. He opened the door and stood there in his nightcap, the legal paper in his hand.

"Told you I'd get your farm one way or t'other, McBroom! It's dawn by the clock and that powerful rich, git-up-and-git acre is all mine!"

"Yup, it's dawn," I said. "No arguing that, Heck Jones. And there's my end of the bargain."

When he saw that crop of tomatoes he just about swallowed his teeth. His mouth puckered up tighter'n bark on a tree.

I took the legal paper out of his hand.

44

"And you bargained to stay off our useless, worn-out one-acre farm, sir. With your hollow cane and your chickens and your muddy shoes and your curled toes. Good day, Mr. Jones."

The young'uns and I all piled into the Popcornmobile to start for home. That's when I saw Princess Prunella. Only she wasn't jumping anymore.

"Merciful powers!" I declared. "Look there! That numbskull cow mistook all this popcorn for snow and has froze to death!"

We got home for a big breakfast and just in time. That prairie dust storm rolled in and stayed for weeks on end. My, it was thick, that dust. Before long our dog was chasing rabbits *up* their burrows. The rodents had dug their holes in the air.

And Heck Jones didn't have any more

sense than to climb up on his barn roof and start shingling over the holes Princess Prunella had made. He couldn't see what he was doing until the wind took a shift and the dust cleared. That's when he saw he'd nailed shingles eight feet out in the dust. They all came tumbling down, but he didn't get hurt. Fell into the tomatoes.

Now it's true — I did tell a lie once. That cow of his didn't *really* freeze to death in all that popcorn. But she did catch a terrible cold.